Join
Super Soccer Boy
online:

www.supersoccerboy.com

Piccadilly Press

For Joan

First published in Great Britain in 2009 by
Piccadilly Press, a Templar/Bonnier publishing company
Deepdene Lodge, Deepdene Avenue, Dorking, Surrey RH5 4AT
www.piccadillypress.co.uk

Text and illustration copyright © Judy Brown, 2009

ISBN: 978 1 84812 042 6

3 5 7 9 10 8 6 4

Printed and bound by CPI Group (UK) Ltd, Croydon, CR0 4YY
Cover design by Simon Davis
Cover illustration by Judy Brown
Text design by Simon Davis

Mixed Sources
Product group from well-managed
forests and other controlled sources
www.fsc.org Cert no. TT-COC-002227
© 1996 Forest Stewardship Council
FSC

Chapter One

The Very Beginning

This is Harry Gribble.

Harry is nuts about football. He'll play anywhere, any time, come rain or shine.

COME ON, HARRY. I'M GETTING SOAKED!!

THE BOY IS A TOTAL NUTTER...

And if he's not playing, he's watching football on TV or reading about his favourite players. Harry can tell you *anything* you want to know (or anything you don't for that matter) about any player in the league, past and present.

There's only one problem — Harry is rubbish at football. In fact, it has been said by his grandad (not when Harry could hear him, of course), that he couldn't kick his way out of a paper bag.

Every Saturday though, whatever the weather, Harry plays 'Little League' in the park around the corner. His dad runs the team that Harry plays in, which is a really good thing because otherwise he might not get to play. You see, although they all like Harry, some of the other

kids don't always want him in their team because, like I said before, he really is rubbish at football.

But Harry doesn't mind what other people think – he just loves to play and, as he says to his dad, 'You never know, *one* day I might play for England.'

One Saturday, after a particularly
nail-biting game of football
when Harry almost (well, not
really almost) scored the
winning goal, Harry and
his dad were walking
back from the park.

'Did you see
my shot, Dad?!'
said Harry. 'It was
SO close, it must
have missed the bar
by millimetres.'

'Hmm, well maybe,
Harry,' said Dad.
'But I don't think it
was *that* close.'

Dad decided to change the subject. 'Look at
the colour of that sky, Harry! Looks like there's
a storm on the way.'

'I hope so!' said Harry. 'I LOVE thunder.'

They turned the corner of Crumbly Drive and walked down to number 49.

'Are you going to watch the match this afternoon?' Dad asked.

'Oh yes!' Harry answered. 'It should be wicked. Whoever wins will go top and did you know that in the last three seasons they've played each other, they've scored a total of twenty-five goals between them, so it's going to be a . . .'

Mr Gribble's mind drifted off as Harry continued to rattle out a whole load more statistics. They walked up the path to the front door. 'Time for lunch, I think!' he said.

An hour later, Harry sat in front of the TV eagerly awaiting kick-off with Ron (short for Ronaldo, of course), his pet rat, by his side as usual. The sky was even darker now and Harry could hear distant rumbles of thunder.

'Here it comes, Ron,' he

said looking out of the window. 'Looks like it's going to be a biggy!'

PEEP! The referee on TV blew his whistle and instantly Harry was gripped by the game.

Now I know that some people believe that animals have a sixth sense when it comes to strange things happening, and it's true that Ron's behaviour was a little odder than usual, but Harry just put it down to the storm. Ron's whiskers were sticking out as stiff as barbecue skewers. He scuttled over to the window and pressed his paws on the glass, his nose twitching crazily. Huge, heavy drops of rain battered against the window panes.

'It's OK, Ron, it's only a thunderstorm,' said Harry. 'Come back and sit by me.'

Ron jumped down and ran away from the

window as the whole room lit up — as if someone had just taken a flash photo. A huge bang shook the house. It shook Harry too, and he stood up to go and get Ron, whose fur was all standing on end. But as he did so, there was an even more blinding flash, then the biggest thunderclap Harry had ever heard.

The lightning had struck Harry's house!

It whizzed and crackled down the aerial and through the TV until . . . Harry was transformed!

He was no longer plain old Harry Gribble who couldn't even dribble. He had become . . .

SUPER SOCCER BOY

In an instant, he somehow knew that he could kick a ball enormous distances with pinpoint accuracy, dribble as fast as a speeding bullet, shoot for goal with the power of a rocket, head the ball like no one's ever seen and do keepy uppy till the cows came home.

Harry's mum burst into the room with his little sister Daisy in tow.

'Harry! Harry! Are you all right?' she asked
frantically.

'Yes, Mum, I'm fine,' said Harry in a dreamy,
far-off voice. 'But I don't think the TV is.'

Mrs Gribble stared at the TV, which was
smouldering quietly in the corner.

Ron stared at Harry, blinking.

Harry just stared into space.

Chapter Two

Harry's Super Skills

Shortly after the storm had passed, the house was full of fire-fighters, electricians, builders and everybody else you call when your house is unlucky enough to have been struck by lightning.

'In future, Madam,' said a very large man with a clipboard, 'I would advise you to unplug your

TV aerial if a storm of this magnitude is passing over. *I* always do.'

'Well, yes, I know that *now*, don't I?' Mrs Gribble snapped. 'Now we have no TV, no fridge or freezer, no computer and a hole in the roof.'

'Power's back on!' said a cheerful–looking electrician, poking his head round the door. 'Not too much damage luckily, so I'll be off.'

'Thank you *so* much,' said Mr Gribble, seeing the man with the clipboard to the door.

Harry sat in the kitchen with Ron, busily eating his way through a tub of ice cream salvaged from the freezer before it went too mushy.

'I feel sort of . . . weird,' he said to Ron. 'Sort of . . . super.'

'Are you sure you're OK?' Mum asked him, bringing Daisy into the kitchen. 'You look a little . . . I don't know . . . odd.'

'No, I'm really great actually,' said Harry. 'Mum? Can I go to the park for a bit? It's nice and sunny now and it'll keep me out of the way of all the workmen.'

Mrs Gribble thought for a moment. 'Yes, I suppose it'd be OK. But not for long, Harry. I think you should have an early night after all this kerfuffle. And anyway . . .'

But before she had the chance to say any more, Harry had grabbed his football, his rucksack and his rat, and disappeared out of the door.

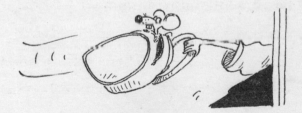

The park was almost empty and Harry was glad. He wanted to see if it was just his imagination or if something amazing had really happened to him.

'Well, Ron,' he said nervously. 'Here goes!'

Harry put his football on the ground and looked at the other side of the park.

'Hmm,' he said to himself. 'I think I'll aim for . . . the sandpit in the kiddy playground.'

Bearing in mind that on any normal day Harry was lucky to kick a ball more than four or five metres and that the sandpit was more like one hundred metres away, you could say that Harry was being a little over-ambitious.

He looked at the ball, then at the sandpit, concentrated hard, took a run up and *WHAM!* The ball flew through the air, straight as an arrow, and landed – *PLOP!* – right in the middle of the sandpit!

'WOW!' said Harry.

What else could he say?

'Wait here,' he said to Ron. 'I'd better go and get it.'

Harry jogged off at normal pace, but suddenly his legs just seemed to take over and before he knew what was happening, he found himself standing in front of the sandpit.

'COOL!' he said looking down at his feet. Absent-mindedly, Harry picked up his football and walked out through the gate of the kiddy playground that he hadn't even noticed vaulting a few moments before.

'I wonder . . .' he said, putting the ball at his feet. Harry closed his eyes for a second, then nudged the ball with the toe of his trainer. You can probably guess what happened next.

Harry put on the most incredible display of dribbling that anyone had ever seen, not that there was anyone apart from Ron there to see it. That didn't matter to Harry though — at that

START

surprised pigeon

bin (poo!)

tree

HARRY'S DRIBBLING DISPLAY (BIRD'S EYE VIEW)

CRISP PACKET

POND

moment, he was the happiest boy on earth.

'Look at me, Ron, I'm brilliant.' He tore round the park with the football at his feet while Ron watched, goggle-eyed. He dribbled in and out of the bushes, around the benches and rubbish bins, right over to the other side of the park.

'WOW!' he said, sitting down next to Ron with a thump. 'I can't wait to show Dad what I can do now!'

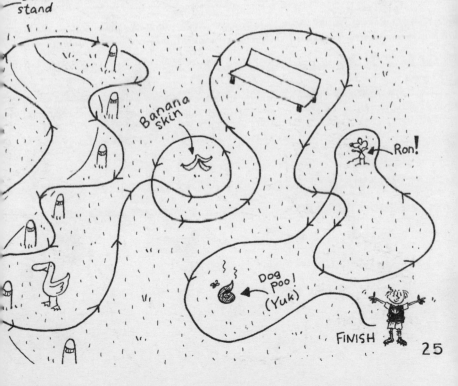

band stand

Banana skin

Ron!

Dog poo! (Yuk)

FINISH

Unfortunately, by the time Harry got home, Dad was in no mood for football, and when Harry suggested they go into the garden for a kickabout, Dad had other plans.

'I'm popping over to Gran's to borrow her old portable until we get our TV replaced. You can come if you want.'

'No, it's OK. I'll just go and practise my keepy-uppies,' said Harry, smiling to himself.

Mrs Gribble started cooking whatever was in the fridge that was going off the quickest and Harry went outside. He was still out there when Dad got back with the TV.

'Is he *still* practising?' asked Dad.

'Yes,' said Mum. 'He seems to be counting for some reason,' she added distractedly.

Mr Gribble looked out of the kitchen window.

'Two thousand seven hundred and one, two thousand seven hundred and two, two thousand seven hundred and three . . .' counted Harry. Harry's dad nearly dropped the TV. He plonked it down on the table. 'Oi! Mind the chicken!' said Mum, moving their dinner out of the way just in time. 'Has Harry been counting ever since I left?'

27

'I think so,' said Mum. 'Why?'

'L-L-Look!' stammered Dad.

There in the garden was Harry, kicking, heading, kneeing and chesting his football to keep it off the ground.

'. . . two thousand seven hundred and fifteen, two thousand seven hundred and sixteen, two thousand seven hundred and seventeen . . . Oh hello, Dad! Oh no! I've lost count. Never mind I guess it must be time for dinner anyway.' He headed the ball into the air one more time, caught it expertly and trotted indoors.

His parents stood in the doorway, speechless.

Chapter Three

Custard Chaos

The next morning, Harry woke with a start.

His first thought was that he'd had a bizarre dream about the house being struck by lightning, but then he heard his mum downstairs telling someone on the phone all about the events of the day before.

'It wasn't a dream then, Ron,' he said to his rat.

Harry's second thought was that the super soccer powers he had suddenly acquired were just a result of the zap from the TV and had probably worn off. Somehow though he didn't think they had.

His third thought was this: 'Hey, Ron, I wonder what happened in that match yesterday? I'd completely forgotten about it!' Harry plucked Ron from his cage and popped him in his pyjama pocket. 'I have to fill in my stats sheets or everything will be out of date!'

He ran downstairs, jumping the last five steps, and burst into the kitchen.

'Dad, what was the score in the match yesterday?'

Dad had a mouthful of toast.

'Didn't you hear?' *Munch, munch.* 'Oh no I
don't suppose you would have. Here, look!'

Mr Gribble handed the Sunday paper to
Harry and pointed to the front page.

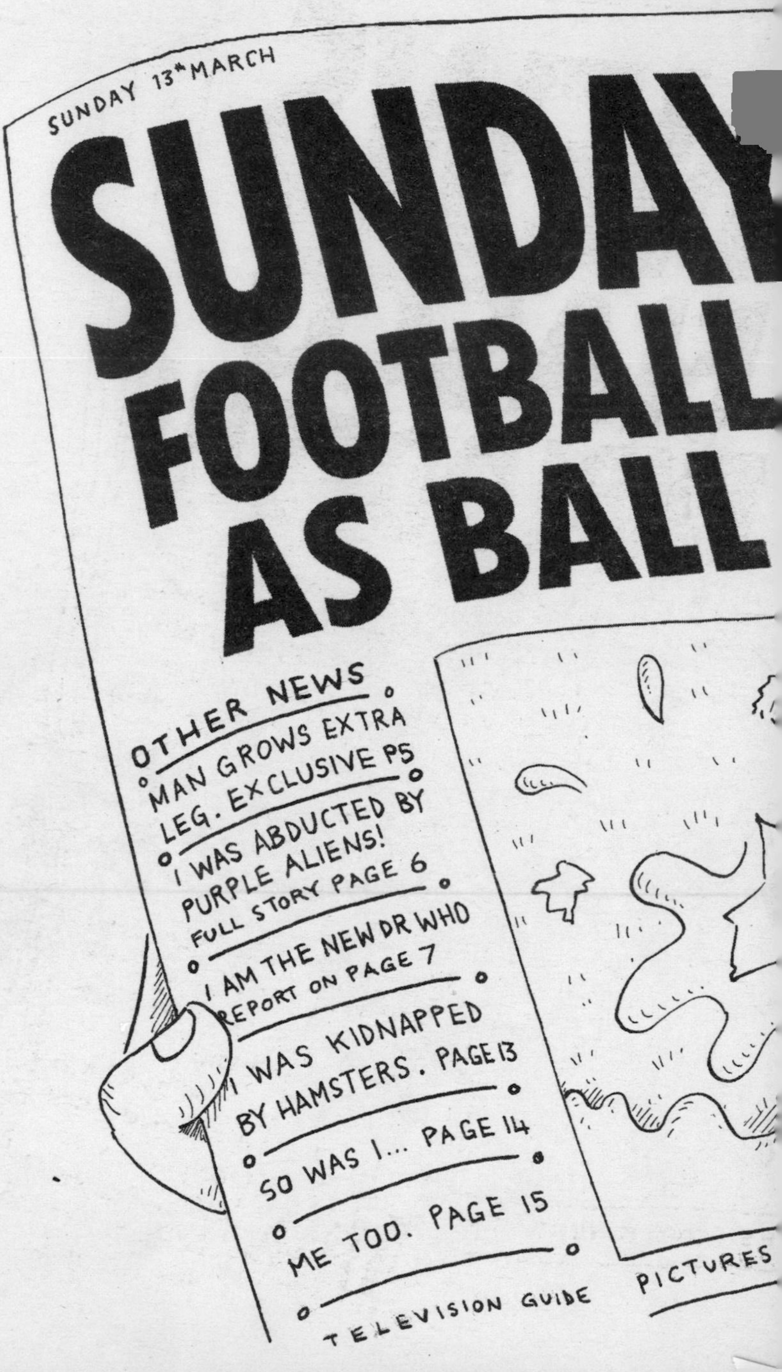
SUNDAY 13th MARCH
SUNDAY
FOOTBALL
AS BALL
OTHER NEWS
MAN GROWS EXTRA LEG. EXCLUSIVE P5
I WAS ABDUCTED BY PURPLE ALIENS! FULL STORY PAGE 6
I AM THE NEW DR WHO REPORT ON PAGE 7
I WAS KIDNAPPED BY HAMSTERS. PAGE 13
SO WAS I... PAGE 14
ME TOO. PAGE 15
TELEVISION GUIDE
PICTURES

NEWS FIASCO EXPLODES!!!

In yesterday's crunch match between the league leaders, all hell broke loose when the match ball exploded just after half-time. No one was injured in the incident but several players were covered in a sticky yellow substance.

'It tasted a bit like custard,' said Emilio Emiliano, the Rovers striker. 'It was a terrible shock!'

One of the United players said later, 'I was as sick as a parrot – I hate custard.'

The match was abandoned when the pitch was deemed unplayable by the referee and his assistants.

ESY OF ROVERS TV

EMILIO EMILIANO

35

'WOW!' said Harry. 'That's the weirdest thing I've ever heard.'

'Isn't it bizarre?' said Mum. 'They've been on about it on TV all morning. Apparently, they've just started using a new football supplier but the police can't track the company down.'

Harry sped into the living room and turned on the TV to see if there was any more news.

'Reports are just coming in,' said the newsreader, 'that another exploding football incident occurred this morning at a premier league training ground. Sally, you're on the scene, what can you tell us?'

'Well, Bill, details are sketchy, but what I *can* tell you is that several players have emerged from the training ground this morning, covered in what I can only describe as custard!' said the reporter excitedly, clutching her microphone.

'I've been trying to get into the ground to find out more, but the police are keeping everybody, apart from staff and players, away from the premises. However, I *have* heard that a white van was seen speeding away just after the incident itself.'

I HATE REPORTERS...

'This is crazy,' said Harry. 'Who would want to sell exploding footballs?'

'The question we are all asking ourselves this morning,' said Bill the newsreader, 'is who would want to sell exploding footballs? And why?' The newsreader stared straight into the camera. 'We'll bring you more news as we hear it.'

Harry turned off the TV and went into the kitchen for breakfast.

'We're going into town to do some shopping after breakfast, Harry,' said Dad. 'We have to order a fridge and stuff, so hurry up and eat your cereal.'

'OK, Dad,' said Harry. 'Dad?'

'Yes, Harry.'

'Why do you think someone would be making footballs explode?'

'Beats me!' said Dad. 'I can think of far better uses of custard. I'm off for a shower. Don't take too long over breakfast, will you?'

Harry looked at Ron and handed him a cornflake. 'It's all very odd, isn't it, Ron?' he said. 'And it's not just *why* someone would do it, it's *how . . .*'

CORNFLAKES... YUM!

Chapter Four

Panic in Middletown

Harry and his family went into town later that morning and had a very boring time, for Harry and his sister anyway, looking at electrical goods. Mind you, it was OK when they were in the shops that sold TVs as it meant that Harry could keep up with what was happening in the news.

As far as Harry could make out, there had

been several more exploding footballs in the same area as the one he'd seen reported that morning.

'The Football Association are to hold an emergency meeting late this afternoon to discuss the situation,' another reporter was saying. 'Meanwhile, in London, the Prime Minister . . .'

Suddenly there was a strange **BOOF!** sound from outside and a **THWUMP!** against the shop window.

'AAAAAARRGGH!' screamed someone in the street.

Everyone in the shop turned to look at the window. It was covered in yellow gunge.

Without even thinking about it, Harry rushed outside.

There was a little boy about three years old standing on the pavement. He was covered head to toe in custard and he was crying his eyes out.

'Oh, my poor baby,' screamed his mum while their dog began to lick the mess off his socks and shoes.

'My b–b–b–ball!' wailed the little boy. 'It sploded. Waaaa!'

'Somebody call the police,' said a voice in the gathering crowd. 'And get the boy a towel!'

'I want my ball!' the little boy blubbered. 'I don't like being yellow and sticky. I want to go home!'

The boy's mum picked him up and cuddled him despite the custard, and he started to calm down.

BOOF! Another weird sound came from further down the street and there was more screaming – and more custard.

'The world's gone mad!' said Mr Gribble, who'd joined Harry outside the shop.

BOOF! BOOFF!! BOOOFFF!!!

A crowd of people came running out of the sports shop on the corner of the high street.

They were all covered in varying amounts of

custard and looking rather shocked. Especially the ones who hadn't heard the news that morning.

It didn't take long after that for the streets to

empty as all the shoppers headed for the car parks and bus stops.

'I think it's time we went home too,' said Mrs Gribble trying not to slip on the custard-covered pavement. 'We've ordered our fridge. Let's get out of this madhouse.'

'Who's doing this?' Harry asked, dismayed.

'Someone who's got a bit of a problem with footballs I would imagine!' said his mum.

It was as if someone had switched on a

lightbulb in Harry's head. Of course! Someone who hates football! If it went on much longer, people would be afraid to play. It would be a disaster!

It was then that he knew. This was a job for . . .

SUPER SOCCER BOY!

Chapter Five

Harry's Super Boots

On the drive home, Harry stared out of the
window in amazement.

'The whole world's covered in custard!' he
said. It was a slight exaggeration maybe, but it
was certainly how it seemed.

Daisy thought it was hysterical. 'Cuspup!
Cuspup!' she roared, watching people slipping all

over the place covered in yellow gloop.

They went past a
local football pitch
where Sunday
league teams
played.

WOOAA!

OOOF!!

The players were trying to play on with another ball after their first one had exploded, but the ground was so slippery they couldn't stay on their feet.

'What they need is special anti-custard football boots,' said Harry thinking out loud.

'Hmm, yes, Harry,' said Dad raising an eyebrow. 'Don't they just.'

But Harry wasn't listening – he'd had an even better idea. What if you could have special boots that you could use in emergencies, like James Bond's car or Batman's utility belt 'Hey, that's it!' he thought. 'Utility boots!'

As soon as they got home, Harry rushed

straight to his bedroom where he spent most of the rest of the day designing his utility boots. Ron watched his every move, fascinated. Harry had always liked making things, but it seemed that now he had Super Soccer powers, his brain had super powers too.

He went into Dad's garden workshop – which everyone else called the shed. It was mostly full of junk, but Harry was looking for bits and pieces that he could use. He found Dad's old laptop which had a broken screen, an old toaster and a box full of springs, nuts and bolts and loads of other bits and pieces. Harry put everything he thought might be useful in a big box and took it back to his room.

Then, Harry made a list of requirements for his utility boots.

1. Extendable studs for super grip.

2. Retractable studs for hard or shiny surfaces (suckers for walking on ceilings?)

3. Wheels. Extra useful for hills + ramps.

4. Skating blades.

5. Turbo – extra speed + height when jumping.

6. Rocket / jet power for flying.

He did drawings and diagrams, made calculations he didn't even know he could do, and worked feverishly well into the night. In fact, it was almost dawn when Harry had finished. He sat back in his chair chuffed to bits with the result. Then he suddenly realised the time.

'Oh dear!' he yawned. 'It'll be time to get up for school in a couple of hours. I'd better have a power nap. I'll try these babies out later.' Harry took one more proud look at his utility boots and crawled under his duvet. He was asleep in seconds.

He had the weirdest dream . . . He was standing with his mum, dad and sister outside the electrical shop, like they had been that morning. The little boy was there, covered in custard, and people were running out of the sports shop down the road. Then everything went into slow motion and Harry noticed a white van driving around the corner away from the high street. There was nothing painted on its side but it had a strange-looking aerial poking out of the top. The man in the van turned towards him and smiled.

Harry knew in an instant that he was looking at the man behind the whole custard catastrophe. He tried to run but it seemed like his feet were stuck to the ground.

'Stop! Stop that van!' he shouted. 'You evil, football-exploding fiend. I'll catch you if it's the last thing I do!'

The next thing Harry knew, his mum was trying to wake him. 'Harry, Harry, what's the matter? You were shouting in your sleep.'

'Was I?' asked Harry groggily.

'It's late, you'd better hurry and get ready for school.' She glanced at his utility boots. 'And get those boots off your desk, it's very unhygienic.'

'Yes, Mum,' said Harry.

He stumbled out of bed, showered, dressed, shoved his utility boots in his schoolbag and sped downstairs, just as his mum was putting toast on the table.

'Thanks,' said Harry grabbing two slices. 'I could eat a horse this morning.'

'Slow down, Harry, you'll give yourself indigestion,' Mrs Gribble told him as he stuffed his face with toast as fast as he could.

'Have to hurry,' Harry said, spraying

bits of toast everywhere. 'Jake'll be waiting for me.'

'Harry! Please don't talk with your mouth full, it's disgusting.'

CHOMP! CHOMP!

'Yuk!' said Daisy as a soggy piece of toast landed on the tray of her high chair. She poked at it with a chubby finger.

'Ooops, sorry!' Harry said, and he washed the rest down with a huge glug of orange juice. 'See you later!' he added and sped to the front door.

'LUNCHBOX!' shouted Mum, throwing it to him as he dashed past.

'Thanks, Mum. Byeee!'

Every morning Harry met his best friend (and Little League team-mate), Jake, at the corner of Crumbly Drive and they walked to school together.

HEY, THAT'S WHERE I SIT. GET OFF!

'Sorry I'm late,' said Harry, arriving in a hurry.

'No worries,' said Jake. 'From what I heard you're lucky to be here at all. My mum said you were nearly barbecued.'

'That's not all that happened,' said Harry with an excited gleam in his eye.

As they walked to school, Harry went on to

tell Jake about his new super skills, footballing and otherwise, then he showed him the utility boots.

'What do you think?' asked Harry proudly.

'I think,' answered Jack, looking a little worried, 'that maybe your brain got barbecued after all. You sure you're feeling OK?'

'Never felt better in my life,' said Harry.

Chapter Six

Evil Ernest

A few miles out of town in an abandoned factory estate, a strange, scrawny man called Ernest Quigley sat in his secret football-making factory. He was looking through that morning's newspapers.

'Look, Tiddles, my plan is working brilliantly!' he squealed, rubbing his hands together.

A large fat cat, who looked as though he should be called anything but Tiddles, waddled over and sat next to him.

Ernest Quigley held up a football and stared blankly as memories of his childhood flooded into his mind.

ERNEST WAS NOT AN ATHLETIC BOY, HE MUCH PREFERRED READING BOOKS AND DOING JIGSAW PUZZLES TO PLAYING FOOTBALL, ESPECIALLY IN THE WINTER.

QUIGLEY! DON'T JUST STAND THERE, RUN. CHASE THE BALL!

ERNEST, MORE SCARED OF THE TEACHER THAN OF THE HORRIBLE WEATHER, SET OFF AS FAST AS HIS WEEDY LITTLE LEGS COULD CARRY HIM.

HEAD IT, ERNEST!

HUH?

THE BALL HURTLED TOWARDS HIM LIKE A BIG, MUDDY COMET.

YURRCH!

UNFORTUNATELY HE'D BEEN SO BUSY HOLDING UP HIS SHORTS, HE HADN'T NOTICED THAT HIS LACES WERE UNTIED.

OH NO! MY SHORTS.

WHAT A NUMPTY!

A loud *PING* brought Ernest out of his memories.

'A-ha!' he said. 'Another batch of footballs ready for filling.'

Ernest had already designed four types of exploding football and had just finished his work on a fifth.

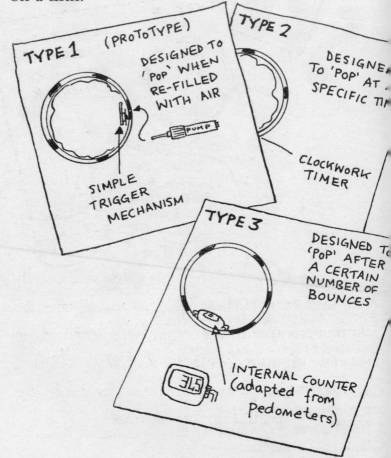

TYPE 1 (PROTOTYPE)
DESIGNED TO 'POP' WHEN RE-FILLED WITH AIR
PUMP
SIMPLE TRIGGER MECHANISM

TYPE 2
DESIGNE TO 'POP' AT SPECIFIC TI
CLOCKWORK TIMER

TYPE 3
DESIGNED T 'POP' AFTER A CERTAIN NUMBER OF BOUNCES
INTERNAL COUNTER (adapted from pedometers)

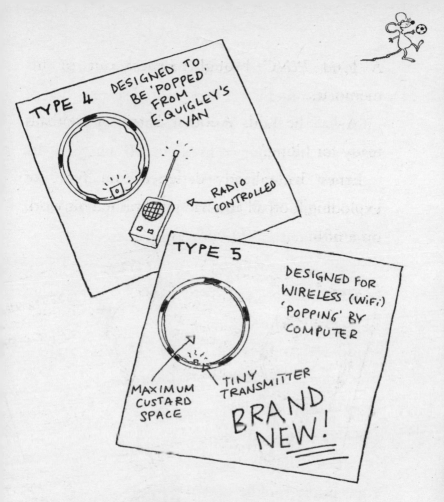

TYPE 4 — DESIGNED TO BE 'POPPED' FROM E.QUIGLEY'S VAN

← RADIO CONTROLLED

TYPE 5

DESIGNED FOR WIRELESS (WiFi) 'POPPING' BY COMPUTER

MAXIMUM CUSTARD SPACE

TINY TRANSMITTER

BRAND NEW!

The balls themselves looked and felt exactly like any other. Ernest had cleverly distributed them throughout the country by setting up several internet football suppliers, offering special discounts to new customers. He'd also been very careful to cover his tracks.

'Hmm. Now to decide on today's route.'

Ernest's memory stick stored every bit of information about his exploding footballs and he never let it out of his sight. He plugged the memory stick into the computer and the location of every single unexploded football he'd sold appeared as little dots on his screen.

'Let's see . . . where to next . . . Ooh, ooh, I haven't done a school yet! And there's one only a few miles away. Rushy Meadow. Lovely! With a bit of luck they'll be right in the middle of football practice now. Mwahahahaha!'

Rushy Meadow just happened to be Harry's school.

Chapter Seven

A Field of Custard

The only topic of conversation at Rushy Meadow that Monday was the weekend's custard chaos.

'We've got tickets for next Saturday's game and my mum says we can't go now 'cos it's too dangerous. It's only custard!' moaned Jason.

'Well, I heard the news this morning and they

said the F.A. might cancel all games until further notice,' said Navir.

Harry was horrified. 'They can't do that! The whole season will be ruined,' he yelled.

'At least they haven't cancelled the games lesson,' said Jake happily.

There was a bit of a pause and a few nervous glances.

'You don't think . . .' Jake's voice trailed off and his smile disappeared.

'Come on, Year Six, hurry up, you're *so* slow. I want you out on the field in two minutes,' said Mr Blunt, the games teacher.

Suddenly though, a lot of them had gone off the idea of games completely.

'Sir?' said Amy, digging the toe of her shoe into the ground. She didn't even like it when a balloon popped, let alone a football. 'Couldn't we play rounders today?'

Several classmates nodded enthusiastically. Harry stepped forward and turned to them angrily. 'Don't you see that's what someone wants?!' he said. 'Are you all chicken? This is our national game, our heritage!'

'Steady on, Harry,' whispered Jake.

'That's the spirit, Harry!' said Mr Blunt. 'Come on, you wimps, put out the cones and let's do some dribbling practice.'

They gingerly started to arrange the cones and even more gingerly carried the footballs from the P.E. cupboard.

'Right. Sort yourselves into groups of four. One ball each.'

They lined up sheepishly and began the dribbling exercise and everything went fine . . . to begin with.

Meanwhile, Ernest Quigley climbed into his white van and put the school address into his sat nav.

'E.T.A. ten minutes. Perfect,' he said with an evil grin. 'Off we go!'

He drove unnoticed — well, his white van

looked pretty much like any other white van. If you looked really carefully though, you *might* see that the aerial was a little ... unusual. As he drove up to the school, Ernest saw that they were in the middle of football practice. He was almost beside himself with glee.

'Oh, oh, how EXCITING!' he squealed. 'This is going to be *so* much fun. I'll have to stay and watch.'

He parked where he would be able to see, but still make a quick getaway. Then Ernest sat and watched for a few

minutes, waiting for exactly the right moment to press the button.

The games lesson was going well. Harry amazed everyone with his much-improved skills. He wasn't trying his *absolute* best though – he didn't think they were ready for that.

'You've certainly improved a lot since Saturday morning,' said Jake. He was beginning to wonder if Harry's fantastic story was really true. But Harry stopped suddenly and stared wide-eyed at Jake.

'What's the matter?' asked Jake, worried.

'I think,' said Harry, 'I think something's about to happen. TAKE COVER!'

There was the now familiar **BOOF!** sound and the first of the footballs exploded. Amy Carter had been about to start her dribbling run but now she was covered head to toe in custard and little bits of exploded football.

'Eeeeeeeck!' There was a collective scream as the entire class began to run for the changing rooms.

But it was too late.

The rest of the footballs exploded one by one and everyone was sliding about in custard. Everyone except Harry that was.

Harry found he could sense which ball was next to explode and with the nimblest display of footwork anyone had ever seen, he wove his way between them, avoiding all of the slippery, messy custard.

'Everybody inside,' shouted Mr Blunt, slipping over and landing in an especially large puddle.

'Look!' said Harry. He'd seen Quigley's white van.

Harry darted between the pools of custard. 'It's the white van they talked about on the news,' he called back, weaving his way across the field. 'I dreamed about it too!'

Inside the van, Ernest Quigley was crying with laughter. 'Tee hee hee hee. Look at them!

Hee hee, it's hilarious,' he guffawed, wiping his face with a large hanky. Then he noticed Harry charging towards him.

'Ooops! Time to go,' he said. He started the van and sped off.

But Harry's super legs sped him across the field. 'Stop that VAN!' he yelled, tearing along the fence that separated the field from the road. But nobody could — they were busy with the custard.

'Rats!' said Harry. 'I'm going to lose him.'

'Try your boots,' said Jake, running out of the changing room with Harry's bag.

'Brilliant!' said Harry. He changed direction and ran towards Jake.

'The van will be stuck in the high street traffic for a while with a bit of luck,' said Jake as Harry changed into his utility boots. 'That's the way it was heading, anyway.'

'Thanks, Jake,' said Harry. 'Here goes.'

Harry got to his feet, clipped the control panel to his football shorts and pressed *Turbo*. With a *whooosh* he was gone, leaving Jake and his custard-covered classmates in stunned silence.

Chapter Eight

Lost and Found

Harry whizzed out of the school gates at turbo speed and turned on to Middletown high street. Way up ahead in front of the traffic lights, he could see Quigley's van.

'Hey you! You in that van, stop!' he yelled. 'It's the football fiend, stop him!'

'Get out of the road, kid,' shouted an angry

motorist. 'You'll get yourself run over.'

Harry realised that this was probably true. He changed course and went on to the pavement.

'Sorry! Ooops! Excuse me,' he said as he tried to weave around the shocked pedestrians.

Ernest Quigley looked in his rear view mirror at the small boy, clad in football kit, who was still chasing him.

'What the . . . Who is that boy? And how is he going so fast?'

By the time the traffic lights had begun to change, Harry had nearly caught up. Quigley

sped off, tyres screeching, but still Harry
followed.

'How on earth is he keeping up?' puzzled
Quigley. He glanced at Harry's boots in the
mirror. 'Those are clearly no ordinary football
boots. This boy could cause me problems.' Then
he smiled. 'But not for long . . .'

Quigley screeched round the corner, off the

main high street, opened the window and launched a football through it. Harry followed but was going so fast that before he had a chance to avoid it, Quigley detonated the football.

It burst right at Harry's feet sending him skidding into a garden hedge.

'Rats!' said Harry, trying to scramble out of the tangle of twigs and branches. 'I really have

lost him this time,' he said as the van disappeared with a puff of exhaust fumes. 'Hang on, though!'

A couple of doors down, Harry noticed a window cleaner's ladder. The window cleaner was just going off for a clean bucket of water.

''Scuse me, won't be a moment,' said Harry squeezing past. In a flash he was up high.

'Oi you!' said the window cleaner. 'Get down from there. You're not insured.'

OI YOU! GET DOWN FROM THERE. YOU'RE NOT INSURED.

Harry looked into the distance and spotted Quigley's van right away.

'So that's where you're going,' he said to himself. 'I've got you now.'

Harry trotted home to find Jake waiting outside with Harry's schoolbag.

'What happened?' asked Jake.

'He got away,' said Harry. 'But I think he's hiding at the abandoned factory estate outside town. I bet that's where he's making the footballs.'

Jake was clearly impressed.

'I'm going there tonight and I'm going to catch him red-handed,' Harry said.

'Can I come too?' Jake blurted out, then instantly began to wonder if he really wanted to.

WHAT ON EARTH DID I SAY THAT FOR?

'If you're sure you want to,' said Harry. 'We'll have to sneak out after dark and go on our bikes. I'll bring Ron along – he may be able to help. Be at the corner of Crumbly Drive at ten, OK?'

'OK!' answered Jake. He felt nervous already.

★ ★ ★

'How was school?' asked Mum when she opened the front door.

'Rubbish,' said Harry. 'All our footballs exploded.'

'Oh dear,' said Mum. 'According to the news, footballs have been exploding randomly all over the country.'

Harry looked depressed. 'Don't worry,' Mum said kindly. 'I'm sure that someone will get to the bottom of it all soon.'

You bet I will, thought Harry.

He went upstairs to get Ron and then sat down in front of Nan's old portable TV to see if there was any more news.

'There were also unconfirmed reports of a

tornado in the Middletown high street. And now,' said the newsreader, 'back to our top story. Footballs have been exploding randomly all over the country. There have even been a few isolated

incidents in France and Holland. It now seems that some of the footballs contain different mechanisms, but at this stage police have no idea where these bogus footballs are coming from. A school in Middletown was closed early today when a game was disrupted by custard.'

'Mum, Mum, my school's on TV,' called Harry.

Mum came running. Daisy toddled after her.

Mr Blunt appeared on TV, still with custardy remnants in his hair. 'It was horrible,' said the teacher. 'The nasty, sticky stuff was everywhere. It'll takes ages to clear it up. Someone needs to sort this business out before people get hurt.'

Harry felt a surge of pride. 'Super Soccer Boy
to the rescue!' he said under his breath.

'What did you say, Harry?' asked Mum.

'Oh, nothing,' he replied.

'Cuspup!' said Daisy pointing at the TV.

Chapter Nine

Quigley's Fiendish Football Factory

After dinner and some keepy uppy practice in the garden, Harry went on the computer to make sure he knew the route to the factory estate. Ron the rat sat on the edge of the keyboard.

'Look, Ron, that's where we're going. It's been empty for years.'

Harry packed his torch and a pair of wire

cutters from the garage into a small backpack, put on his utility boots and outfit and sat in his room waiting for ten o'clock.

At ten on the dot, he crept past Daisy's room (she was fast asleep and snoring happily), down the stairs and past the front room where Mum and Dad were watching some boring programme on TV.

He opened the door quietly and slipped out into the night. There was almost no moon so it was quite dark despite the streetlamps. It was chilly too. Harry had left his bike in the front garden earlier on that evening and he pushed it out of the front gate and pedalled to the corner. Jake had just turned up. He looked really nervous.

'Are you OK?' asked Harry. 'I'll go on my own if you like.'

'It's OK,' said Jake attempting to smile. 'I'll be fine once we get going, it's just that I've never done anything like this before.'

'Me neither,' said Harry riding off.

'Is that supposed to make me feel better?' Jake wondered.

Harry followed the map he'd printed out and, as they got closer to their destination, they began to pass boarded up warehouses with demolition signs. There were old wrecked cars, broken shopping trolleys and piles of rubbish. Ron sank down further inside Harry's backpack — it was pretty scary.

WARNING HAZARDOUS SUBSTANCES NO TRESPASSING

DANGER DEMOLITION WORK IN PROGR

'Stop!' said Harry, suddenly.

'What?' said Jake with a wobble in his voice.

'I can hear *The Sound of Music*,' Harry said.

'Huh? What kind of music?' asked Jake.

'No. I mean I can hear *The Sound of Music*, you know, the musical. Someone must be listening to it in that old factory.' Harry pointed. 'Sounds like . . . "Edelweiss" to me. Yuk.'

'I can't hear a thing,' said Jake. *Apart from my knees knocking together and my teeth chattering*, he thought.

'Over there! It must be him!' Harry said eagerly.

They got off their bikes and followed the chain-link fence on foot for a while until they came to a gate.

'Look!' said Harry. 'It's got a shiny new padlock – this *must* be it.' He peered through the fence. 'Hey, there's the van. What a result! We just need to find a way in.'

The wire cutters Harry had brought were nowhere near big enough to cut through the fence. They followed it round and, after a few minutes, Harry and Jake spotted a hole just about big enough to squeeze through. Unfortunately though, they didn't spot the CCTV camera that was watching their every move ...

As soon as it saw them, warning lights began to flash in Ernest Quigley's office, where he was enjoying a cup of cocoa. Tiddles was on his third bowl of custard.

'A-ha!' said Quigley. 'What have we here, Tiddles? Little visitors?' He zoomed in with the infra-red camera. 'And it looks like they've brought a little snack for you!'

Chapter Ten

The Break-In

Harry and Jake ran over to an old storage shed.

'Don't you think we should just call the police?' asked Jake.

'We've not really got much to tell them yet and why would they listen to us, anyway? We need evidence first,' Harry said. 'Did you bring your mobile?'

'Yes, Harry.'

'Great. You wait here and if I don't come out in an hour – call the police.'

Jake breathed a huge sigh of relief. 'Are you sure you'll be OK alone?' he asked.

'I'll be fine. Anyway, I'm not alone – I've got Ron with me. Besides, I'm Super Soccer Boy, aren't I?'

'Er, yes, I guess so,' replied Jake.

As Harry left the shed, Quigley was watching him on his monitor.

PHEW!

'Hey, don't I know that boy?' he said. 'Wasn't he the one that . . . Hey! Where did he go?!'

Harry had darted off at super-speed towards the factory. Quigley frantically turned the camera around to see where he'd gone, but Harry was too fast. He and Ron were now in a small loading bay where the white van was parked. Harry wiped a dirty window and looked into the building.

'Can't see a thing, Ron.' He fumbled in the backpack for his torch and shone it through the window. 'Wow!'

Harry saw a huge room and there were piles and piles of boxes labelled *Footballs*.

'There must be thousands of footballs in there. But how do we get in?'

Harry shone the torch around the window. There was a small piece of glass missing from the frame. It wasn't big enough for Harry to get through, but it was just big enough for Ron.

'If you can get through that hole, Ron, you could unlatch the window for me.'

Ron's whiskers twitched. He knew what Harry wanted him to do. In a flash he was through the window and, with a bit of strain, up popped the latch.

'Yesss!' said Harry punching the air. He pushed open the window and climbed in.

Just as Harry stepped foot in the room, *The Sound of Music* stopped, right in the middle of 'Climb Every Mountain'. Over the other side of the room, a shaft of light appeared in the gloom as the door of

the main office opened. Ernest Quigley
emerged with Tiddles waddling behind him,
whiskers dripping with custard. He shut the
office door. There was a loud *click* and the
entire room was illuminated.

Now Harry could see everything properly. At his end of the huge room were the boxes of footballs. The office that Quigley had come from was up a flight of steps on the right hand side, and nearby were hundreds of cartons of eggs, boxes of sugar and a large tank labelled *Milk*.

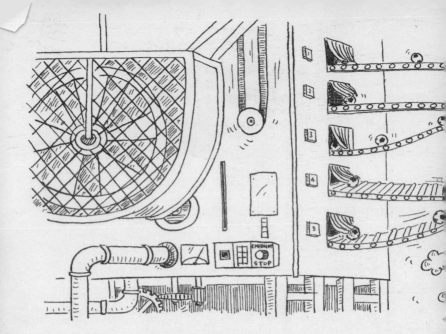

The rest of the room was filled with machinery. From what Harry could make out, one of the machines was for making footballs and it seemed to have five separate conveyor belts coming off it. Another machine had some sort of high pressure hose attached. Harry followed the line of the hose with his eyes as it snaked around the room until he saw at the far end ... an absolutely enormous vat.

There was a little steam coming from the top of it, and the unmistakable smell of custard in the air.

'Helloooo!' Quigley called in a sing-songy voice.

Harry and Ron flattened themselves against a line of boxes.

'I know you're there,' he chuckled. 'Come out, come out, wherever you are!' Quigley carried on walking down the steps from the office. 'Tiddles can smell your furry little friend you know. And – he's – HUNGRY!'

Harry stiffened. He didn't know what to do!

Chapter Eleven

Harry v. Quigley

Harry tried to think. How could he use his super skills to get him out of this sticky situation?

The first thing to do was to make sure Ron was safe. He picked Ron up, climbed a pile of boxes and put him on the top. 'That fat lump of fur will never reach you up here. Stay out of sight.'

Then Harry took out the wire cutters and cut down the side of one of the boxes. He pulled out a football, ran to the end of the room and drop-kicked it a full twenty metres. It landed right on top of Ernest Quigley's head.

'Ow!' he complained. 'That hurt. Why, you little . . .' Quigley ran towards Harry meaning to grab him. 'I'll get you for that.'

Harry was way too fast though, and he disappeared back behind the rows of boxes.

'The game's up!' shouted Harry.

'Oh no it isn't!' sneered Quigley. He began to move along the line, pushing boxes of footballs, causing the towers of boxes to tumble. Ron was standing on one of them and was nearly crushed as it fell, but he jumped to the safety of the windowsill just in time.

'You won't get away with it, not now we know where you are,' said Harry, ducking and weaving, trying not to get buried in footballs.

'Hah! I'll just go and set up somewhere else. All the information I needed is on this memory stick and you'll never get your nasty little hands on it!'

SQUEAK!

'I wouldn't be so sure about that. I'll find it somehow,' Harry replied.

'It won't do you any good. My new design of exploding footballs will be all over the world by now. I can set them off whenever I want to with the touch of a button. Once I've got rid of you, nothing can stop me.'

'You're mad!' yelled Harry.

'Very possibly!' laughed Quigley, maniacally.

By now there were hundreds of footballs bouncing all over the place and as Quigley reached the end of the line of boxes, Harry was there waiting. He fired ball after ball at Quigley with his powerful left foot.

'Oww! Oooh! Oh! Stop that, you're hurting me,' moaned Quigley. He turned and ran, but not to hide – he went to grab the hose. 'You might be fast,' taunted Quigley, 'but you can't run through custard! Mwahaha!'

He switched on the hose and tonnes of custard spewed on to the factory floor, turning it into a big sticky mess.

'That's where you're wrong, Mr Quigley,'
announced Harry. He pressed a button on his
control pad. 'I think this calls for super suckers!'
he said triumphantly.

Little rubber suckers popped out of the soles
of his utility boots and he ran through the
custard as if it wasn't there.

'NO!' yelled Ernest Quigley, retreating up the steps to his office. He pointed the hose directly at Harry but it didn't slow him down. 'You won't get me, you WON'T!'

'GIVE ME THAT MEMORY STICK!' shouted Harry.

'NEVER!' said Quigley as he dropped the hose and grabbed some eggs, throwing them at Harry as he followed him up the steps.

But Harry skilfully caught them and threw them back.

Quigley was now covered in custard, and eggs too, but unlike Harry he didn't have super suckers on his shoes. He was slipping and sliding as he backed away. Harry was advancing ever closer to grab Quigley's memory stick.

'Stay away from me!' said Quigley, moving backwards and not noticing that he'd almost reached the end of the walkway. At last, his long spidery legs lost their footing completely, he tipped back over the rail, *PLOP!* Right into the huge vat of custard.

'Oh no, the memory stick!' said Harry as Quigley fell. He darted forward at super speed, and pulled the stick from around Quigley's neck just before it joined him in the custard.

'Phew!' said Harry. 'That was a close one!'

Chapter Twelve

Extra Time

Moments later, Harry heard sirens. Jake had heard the kerfuffle and called the police already.

'Help! Help! I can't swim!' called Quigley from the vat, as the police broke in. A police officer in wellies helped Quigley out of the vat, and he was led away, all yellow and soggy.

'You'll be needing this, officer,' said Harry,

anding over the memory stick. 'I think it'll tell you everything you need to know.'

'Er, thank you, young man,' said the officer.

There was quite a lot of explaining to do when Harry got home but, although he was in trouble for going out at night without telling anyone, his mum and dad were very proud of him.

Better still, a few weeks later, Harry had an unexpected letter. It was addressed to *Super Soccer Boy*.

'Cool!' said Harry when he opened the envelope. Inside were four V.I.P. tickets to the F.A. Cup Final!

HARRY'S FOOTBALL FACTS!

In 1890 a Mr Brodie from Liverpool invented the goal net.

The first year of British League football was 1888.

The arch at Wembley Stadium weighs the same as 10 Jumbo Jets.

Brazil have been in more world cup finals than any other nation (and they've won more!)

King Carol II of Romania personally selected his country's team for the 1930 world cup.

The first ever world cup game was on 13th July 1930. It was FRANCE v MEXICO

Referees can run up to **8** miles in a single football match!

The highest ever score in a world cup qualifier was 31-0 on 11th April 2001. Australia v American Samoa

The first Women's World Cup was won by the USA.

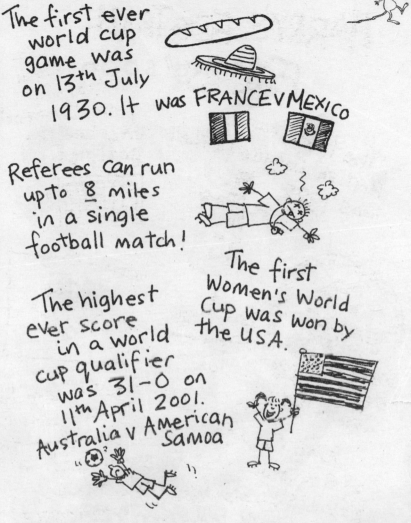

In 1872 the size of footballs used in matches was agreed.

Coming soon

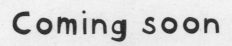